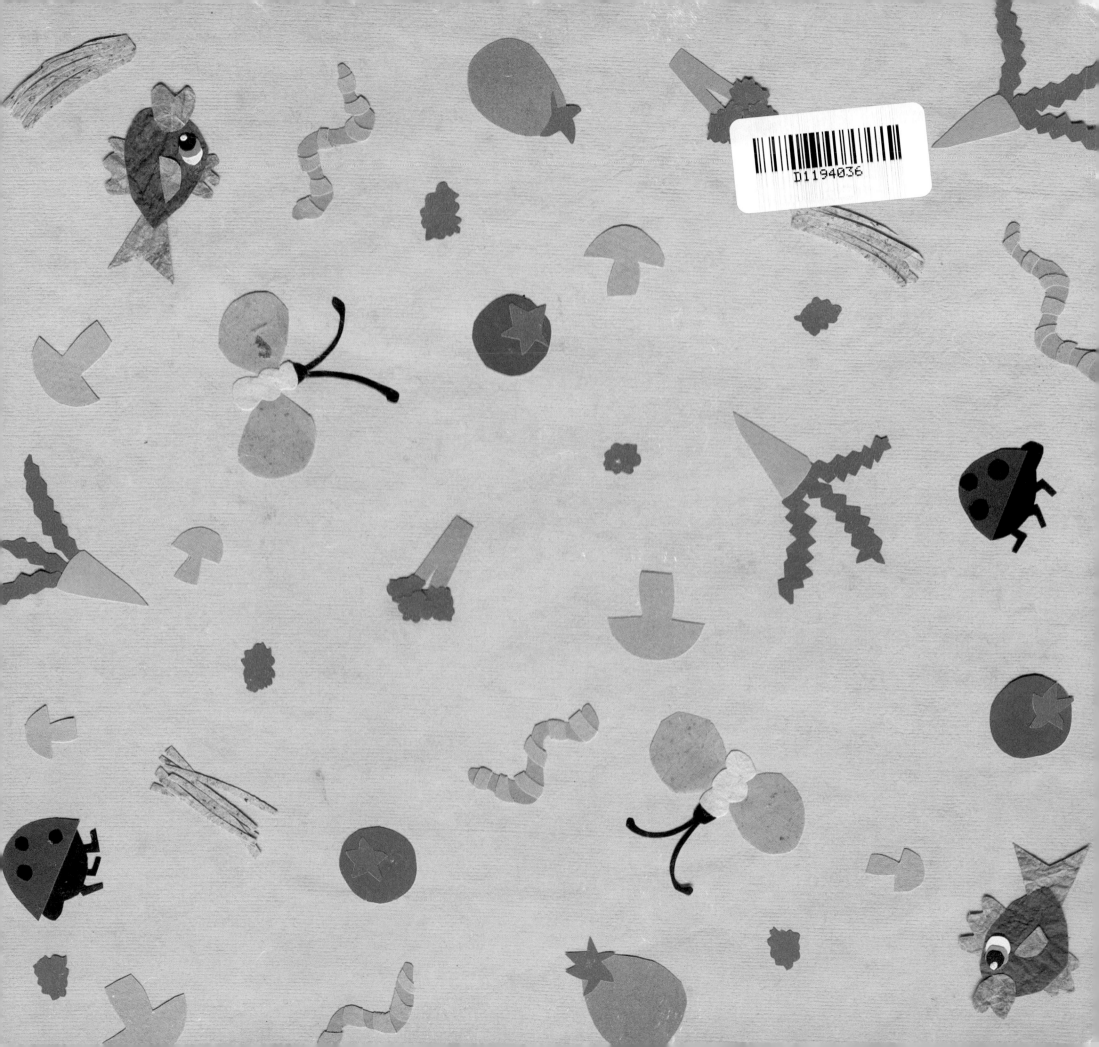

To Margery, for her support and guidance.
Special thanks also to Blake.

—D.D.

# Veggie Soup

Donohue, Dorothy D.
Veggie Soup / written and illustrated by Dorothy Donohue.
First Edition
p. cm.
Summary: Miss Bun, a rabbit who loves to cook, gets help from Bird, Cat, Toad, and
Cow in making a very unusual veggie soup.
ISBN 1-890817-21-x
[1. Soups–Fiction. 2. Cookery–Fiction. 3. Rabbits–Fiction. 4. Animals–Fiction.]
1. Title.
PZ7.D72233 S1                    2000
[E]–dc21
99-46307        CIP

**Creative Director: Bretton Clark**
**Editor: Margery Cuyler**

Printed in Belgium

This book has a trade reinforced binding.

# Veggie soup

*written and illustrated by*

# Dorothy Donohue

## WINSLOW PRESS

**Delray Beach, Florida • New York**

For games, links and more, visit our interactive Web site:
**winslowpress.com**

Miss Bun liked to
cook. Being a rabbit, she
especially liked to cook
dishes with vegetables.
Her corn chowder, carrot
cake, cabbage crunch,
potato pudding, and
barbecued broccoli had
won first prizes in cooking
contests. All of her dishes
were made from recipes
in Great Nana's wonderful
cookbook.

Toad

But one day Miss Bun felt like creating her own recipe. "Something tasty, something original, something all my own...veggie soup!" she decided. "I'll make the very best soup in the whole wide world and invite my friends to try it. I'll have a veggie soup party!"

Miss Bun filled a big purple pot with water. She set it on the stove. As she waited for it to boil, she skipped around the room and sang:

*Water, water,*
*cold to hot,*
*simmer, boil*
*in the pot.*

Just then, Crow cawed at the window.

"Hi, Crow," said Miss Bun. "Are you coming for dinner?"

"Oh yes," answered Crow, "and I have brought you a very special crow treat. Some wiggly worms! They will be just right in your soup."

"But I am making veggie soup. Wiggly worms aren't vegetables!" cried Miss Bun.

"Just call it Veggie Soup with Worms," cawed Crow as he flew away.

Miss Bun set the wiggly worms aside. Then she washed and dried the vegetables and cut them up. As she chopped, she sang:

*Wash and dry,*
*cut and chop,*
*onions fly,*
*green beans pop.*

Just then Cat meowed at the window.

"Hi, Cat," said Miss Bun. "Are you coming for dinner?"

"Oh yes," meowed Cat, "and I have brought you a very special cat treat. Some tangy tunas. They will be tasty in your soup!"

"But I am making veggie soup. Crow brought me wiggly worms. Now you've brought me tangy tunas. Worms and tuna aren't vegetables!" Miss Bun cried.

"Just call it Veggie Soup with Worms and Tuna," Cat meowed as he ran away.

Miss Bun put the tangy tunas aside. Then she gathered all the chopped vegetables and tossed them into the pot. As she waited for them to boil, she hopped around the room and sang:

*Yellow squash,*
*ripe tomatoes,*
*carrots, beans,*
*red potatoes.*

Just then Toad hopped through the window.

"Hi, Toad," said Miss Bun.
"Are you coming for dinner?"

"Oh yes," croaked Toad,
"and I have brought you
a very special toad treat.
Some beastie bugs. They
will add zest to your soup!"

"But I am making veggie
soup. Crow brought me
wiggly worms. Cat brought
me tangy tunas. Now you've
brought me beastie bugs.
Worms, tuna, and bugs
aren't vegetables!"
Miss Bun cried.

"Just call it Veggie Soup
with Worms, Tuna, and
Bugs," Toad croaked as
he hopped away.

Miss Bun put the bugs aside. She turned down the soup. As it simmmered, she danced around the room and sang:

*Veggies, veggies,*
*simmering hot,*
*swishing, swirling,*
*in the pot.*

She tasted the soup. "This soup is more blaaaa than I expected," she thought. "It needs a little spicing up!" She sprinkled in some spices and stirred them around. She skipped about the room and sang:

*Add some herbs,*
*add some spice,*
*a pinch of sage,*
*would be nice.*

Just then Cow stuck her head through the window.

"Hi, Cow," said Miss Bun. "Are you coming for dinner?"

"Oh yes," mooed Cow, "and I have brought you a very special cow treat. Some homegrown hay! It will be perfect with your soup!"

"But I am making veggie soup. Crow brought me wiggly worms. Cat brought me tangy tunas. Frog brought me beastie bugs. Now you've brought me homegrown hay. Worms, tunas, bugs, and hay aren't vegetables!" Miss Bun cried.

"Just call it Veggie Soup with Worms, Tuna, Bugs, and Hay," Cow mooed as he trotted away.

Miss Bun set the homegrown hay aside. She tasted the soup again.

"Oh!" she groaned. "It is still missing something. And it's time for dinner." Miss Bun frantically looked around the room. "Maybe my friends' special ingredients *would* help." She gathered up all their gifts and dumped them into the soup. Then she bounced around the room and sang:

*Worms and bugs,*
*hay and fish,*
*all I need*
*for a tasty dish.*

KNOCK, KNOCK!
Her dinner guests were at the door.

Miss Bun poured a bit of soup into Great Nana's china bowls. She waited as her guests each took a sip.

"Chirp-ewy!" screeched Crow.

"Mew-yuck!" hissed Cat.

"Ribbit-icky!" croaked Frog.

"Moo-poo!" groaned Cow.

"This is horrible!" yelped Miss Bun. "This is not the very best soup in the whole wide world; it's the very worst!"

She thought for a minute. "I have an idea!" she said.

"Let's make another veggie soup! Only this time we will follow Great Nana's recipe."

"Hooray!" cheered her friends.

Miss Bun read the recipe, and everyone helped.

When the new soup was done, everyone had a bowl. "How do you like it?" asked Miss Bun. "It's soup-perb!" they all cried. All Miss Bun's friends agreed that this soup was better with only veggies. "But look how much is left!" Miss Bun said. Then she had another idea.

### Great Nana's Veggie Soup Recipe
*(Do not make without adult supervision!)*

2 tablespoons olive oil
1 large chopped onion
1 cup chopped potato
1 cup chopped carrots
1 cup chopped broccoli
1 cup chopped celery
3 cups vegetable broth or
    chicken broth
1 teaspoon oregano
1 teaspoon thyme
1 bay leaf
salt and pepper

In a large saucepan, warm the oil over medium heat. Add the onion and stir slightly until it begins to soften (3-5 minutes). Add all the vegetables, the stock, and the herbs and bring to a boil. Reduce the heat and simmer until the vegetables are tender (15-20 minutes).

4-6 servings

A soup kitchen is a place where the needy and hungry go to get free soup. It is run by volunteers.

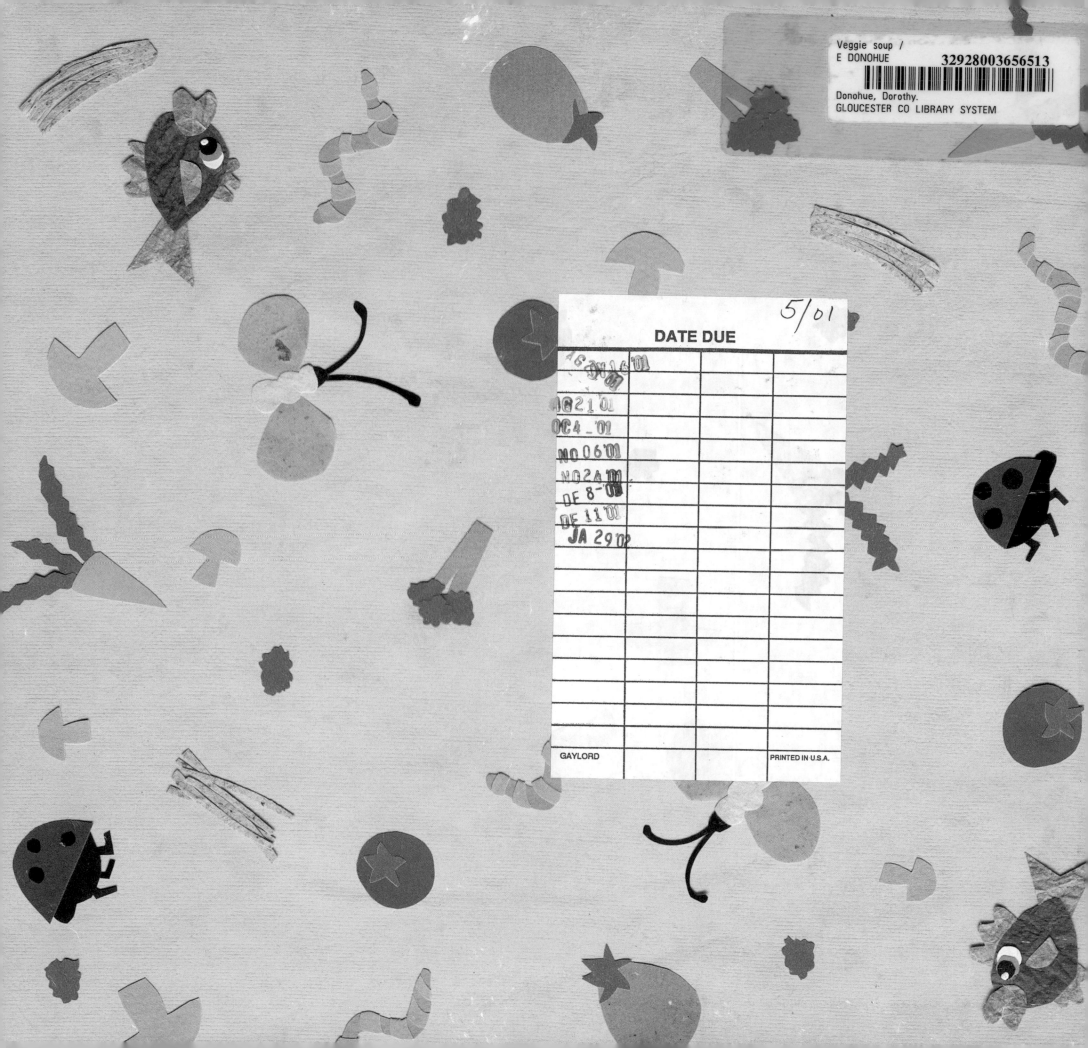